THE WILD ONE

Start Publishing PD is a registered trademark of Start Publishing PD LLC
Manufactured in the United States of America

Cover art: Shutterstock/Taisiya Kozorez

Cover design: Jennifer Do

10 9 8 7 6 5 4 3 2 1

ISBN 979-8-8809-2255-0

THE WILD ONE

by Marion Zimmer Bradley

THE WILD ONE

This is a story that they tell on the solitary farms on the borders of the Catskill mountains, where I grew up. It is a mistake to think that country is settled and modern, just because the big highways stretch from city to city, and the factories hold out clean jobs that pay better than the scratch-the-soil farming on shale rock. For between every farm is a stretch of woodland, and every farm has its own woods, and by night there are deer and rabbits and even wolves and the big lynxes that prowl south of Canada in a hungry season. And every now and again, to some lonely farm-girl who roams the edges and center of the deep woods by night, a child will be born like Helma Lassiter . . .

Roger Lassiter lifted his hands abruptly from the keys of die piano, and stared across the room at his sobbing young wife.

"Helma, dear!" he said contritely, "If I'd known—I didn't hear you come in, dear. Please forgive me?"

"Of course!" Helma wiped away her tears, and her strange, hesitant smile flickered for an instant on the wet face, "If I'd known you wanted to play, I wouldn't have come back so early." She crossed the room, and Roger held out his arms to stop her as she passed and hold her, for a moment, close to him. "Did you and Nell Connor have a good time?"

She dropped her eyes. "I didn't go to see Nell, Roger, it was too lovely hi the woods. And—and there'll be a full moon tonight. ..."

He slid his arm around the girl's waist. "You're the wildest child of nature I ever knew," he murmured, halfway between exasperation and indulgence, and from the piano bench he twisted to look out the window at the deep stretch of dark woodland, oaks and maple and birch, that surrounded their house; then he turned back to rest his eyes on Helma.

She was good to look at; a tawny blonde girl, slight, delicately but strongly made, with creamy skin and dark-gray eyes that lightened to amber or an odd gold-flecked green when she was angry or excited, and so incredibly supple that he often wondered if she had been a ballet dancer. He did not know what she had been; she never talked about her childhood, and he knew only that she had run away from a farm in the Adirondacks when she was only fourteen years old. She had been twenty-three when they met, a chance acquaintance, almost a pick-up, at the swimming pool in Albany. Roger, escorting a pair of frisky nephews, had been attracted, then charmed, by her unbelievable grace in the water, her swift clean beauty; a seal-woman of the legends could have shown herself no more at home in the sea. He had been shocked at the change which had come over her when she had run back to the dressing-rooms and reappeared in a cheap skirt and blouse, her hair brushed down and her legs encased in lumpy socks and shoes. It was as if rust had suddenly covered a bright coin. But he had not been able to forget the laughing, glowing nymph of the pool. And he had never forgotten. It had not taken him long to discover how she revived in the woods, in the country. After their marriage, they had built this small house at the edge of the forest; a necessity, not a luxury, for Helma drooped and wilted in an apartment. They had built the house with their own hands, camping in the woods while it rose from the foundations, sleeping at night in a tent; and day by day a visible radiance had crept over Helma until she seemed alive with an inner, glowing beauty. Still, on the first night they had slept in their new home, she had murmured "I think I liked the tent better!" Even now, for choice, she slept on the open porch when she could.

He smiled now into her half-closed eyes and murmured what he had said many times, "I think you're half wood-cat, Helma!"

"Oh, I am," she returned, as always, "I am. Didn't you know?"

"And say, I used to have a dog who howled just like that when I played the piano. It's not what you'd call a compliment to my playing!"

She colored . . . even after four years of marriage, she was very sensitive about this. "I can't help it," she whispered for the hundredth time, "It hurts my ears so much—"

He patted her shoulder gently. "Well, never mind, honey, I try not to play when you're around," he told her, "but seriously, I'm beginning to wonder if you ought to go so far into the woods alone. Bob Connor told me he's heard wolves, and the other day he shot a lynx. Perhaps it's all right in broad daylight, but I wish you'd stay out of the woods at night, Helma."

He was not a countryman by habit; born and reared in cities, it had thrown him into a panic, the first time that he had waked in the night and found himself alone in bed. He had hunted the house through and found it empty; in a growing apprehension, mounting to absolute terror, he had searched the woods with a lantern, shouting, panicked, until he had finally found Henna, snuggled into a hollow of summer grass, sleeping, a rabbit bolting from her side as he came near.

After a few months he had come to take it for granted; Helma was almost physically incapable of staying out of the woods when they were so near, night or day. Sometimes Roger wondered if he had been wise to bring her so far from the cities and the plowed farms on the highways; she might have been unhappy, but she might have been less wild.

He murmured, "Perhaps if we had a child—"

He had spoken almost under his breath, but her body stiffened in the curve of his arm and she pulled away from him. "Roger," she murmured, "You know I can't—"

He said, low-voiced, "We haven't talked much about this, because it always makes you so unhappy. Now I think we must. How do you know you can't have children? Perhaps we could see Doctor demons when we go into town this Saturday. Perhaps—"

Helma jerked away from him furiously, taut, her head flung back, even the short sleek tawny hair seeming electric and alive, and her eyes flared green. The small blunt hands were flexed into claws. "I won't!" she spat at him, "I won't be mauled about and stared at by some doctor. ..."

"Helma! Roger's sharp voice cut through her hysteria; she relaxed a little, but went on in a low angry voice, "I've never told you much about me, have I? I know that. I can't have your child, such a child as I could have, you wouldn't want, I—" She slumped down on a corner of the divan and buried her face in her arms despondently. After a long time she raised her face. "Would it make you so happy if I had a baby, Roger?" she asked pitifully.

The man could not bear it. He stood up and went to her, seating himself on the divan at her side and pulling the blonde head down on his shoulder. "Not if you don't want to, Helma," he said, in a gentle voice, "Maybe you're right, maybe—"

Her wide eyes burned tearlessly in the twilight. "You think I'm wild, you think I'm a crazy woman who might be normal if I had a baby to tie me down a little bit. You want me to be like your friends' wives, like Nell Connor, sleep in my bed nights and never step out further than the chicken house!" Her voice fell steadily, accusing. She pushed him away from her, stood up and backed away toward the door, a low menace, not quite a word, in her throat. Before her green glare his own eyes fell.

"Well, damn it, Helma," he muttered, "I'd appreciate it if you'd try, at least, to act like a normal adult human being! There are times when you're like a wild animal!"

"I am," she said huskily, and swiftly turned and went out of the room. Half rising, the man saw through the window the quick bound with which she crossed the porch and lawn, watched her bend, with that amazing suppleness, and unfasten first one sandal, then the other. She kicked her feet free and ran toward the back gate; with a single lissome movement she was up and over it, and Roger saw the pale gold of her hair and the green-and-brown plaid of her house dress melt into the forest like a shadow, and there was a tight breathlessness in his throat as he watched her slide away and vanish in the leaves. But she was back before morning, slipping silently, barefoot, through the doors, and sliding into bed beside him, as noiselessly as a cat. Roger, who had not closed his eyes all night, felt her presence and moved toward her, but she shoved him away. Roger shrugged and sighed; he was used to this, too. Helma could be as violent and passionate as a young lioness when aroused, but she was curiously cold at other times, and would push or cuff him away if he touched her when she was not in the mood. Roger had reflected that civilized man alone, of all animals, is not cyclic in desire, and that Hernia's odd wildness was probably nothing more than a reversion to an earlier, possibly a cleaner day. Since in spite of occasional exasperations, Roger loved his wife devotedly, he respected her moods; it was as well that he did, for once, in the first year of their marriage—before he had learned how deep this was ingrained into Helma's whole nature—he had been less tolerant, and had once—only once—attempted to take her by force. There was still a tiny white line across his cheek where her wild hands had raked bone-deep. She had sobbed frenzied apologies afterward, but Roger had never risked it again. All women, he knew, were periodic to some extent; and it was true that she was altogether satisfying when her nature allowed her to be compliant.

In the days and weeks that followed, Helma was unusually quiet, subdued and docile. Summer lazed to a close; the crisp leaves of September drifted from helpless branches and the twanging winds of autumn played mournful threnodies in the deserted woods. Helma haunted the leaf-deep paths by day, but not once did she run off by night, and Roger Lassiter began to wonder if she was actually settling down. Surely it was time, after four years of marriage, that Helma should take on a look of sleekness and content, and for her body to soften a little from its hard angularity. She worked around the house happily—it was always neat and clean, but now it positively shone with soap and wax and polished floors, and Helma herself seemed as smooth and clean as a well-kept cat. Even her quick dancing walk seemed, although just as graceful, a trifle firmer and more subdued. And sometimes in the evenings when Roger returned home ... he worked days, in a chemical factory ... he would hear Helma singing, a curious contralto croon, almost toneless, but rising and falling in smooth, well-defined rhythmic cadences that were sweetly resonant. She never told him, in so many words, that she was pregnant. Roger, although he guessed it as early as September, kept aloof from asking, thinking that perhaps she wanted to tell him herself, when she chose; but she never did, and finally he asked her only "When?" "Early in the spring," she said, and her greeny eyes glanced, half-sorrowful, at his glad face. He told her gently, "You see, you were wrong, Helma. Aren't you happy about this?"

THE WILD ONE

She did not answer, but put down her book and came to curl up on the rug at his feet, putting her head of thick short straight hair into his lap. He stroked it without speaking, and she shut her eyes, leaning against his knee. After a time she began the odd rough contralto crooning, and he smiled. "What kind of witch-chant is that, Helma? I never heard you sing before. I didn't know you knew one note from another."

"I don't," her smile was a gamin, enigmatic thing. "I don't know, I remember hearing my mother sing like this when I was very small."

"What was your mother like?" he asked, and Helma laughed softly.

"Like me."

"I'd like to have seen that! What was your father like?"

She shrugged. "I don't know. Perhaps—someone like you. Perhaps he was—different. Perhaps I never had a father, I can't remember."

Roger persisted "Did your mother never tell you?"

Helma suddenly drew her head away from her husband's stroking hands, looking up at him slantwise through her hair. "You would have called my mother mad," she said evenly, "She said my father was a lynx—a wildcat she called it."

Roger abruptly shivered as if a freezing wind had blown out the cozy fire. "Don't talk rubbish, Helma."

13

She shrugged. "You asked me. It's what my mother used to say. She was mad, madder than I am. She lived on a farm away up in the mountains, with only her grandfather and a little sister. She used to listen to hunters' stories about men and women who turned into wolves and wildcats when the moon was full, and ran in the woods at night. I've heard old men howl like the gray timber-wolf, when the moon lit up the snow like daylight, and seen them slink through the shadows with red eyes. ..."

"Hell! You're morbid tonight!"

"No. Why? When I was a little girl I used to run around the hunters' huts. I could walk along a path and a wildcat would walk along the limb of a tree right over me and never even snarl, and I could pick up rabbits with my bare hands. I still can." Her smile was frankly malicious now. "You don't believe those old stories, do you? Till she died, my mother used to run out in the woods every full moon. She said my father was a lynx, I didn't. Do you believe I'll turn into a wildcat some night and rip out your throat? A silver bullet isn't any good, you know. That's just an old wife's tale. Just an iron knife, a knife of cold iron will kill a turn skin animal. That's what they say. Iron, or lead. Are you afraid of me?" She laughed, and Roger felt his goose fleshed arms stiffen and crawl. "For Godsake, cut it out!" he almost shouted.

She had stiffened and pulled away.

THE WILD ONE

"I'm sorry. You asked me."

Roger Lassiter dreamed that night of wandering in black leafless woods, while green cat-eyes, disturbingly like Helma's, watched him from low branches; she came in before dawn, her dress torn, a bloodstain on one foot, shivering with cold, and lay huddled in warmed blankets, sobbing, while a dismayed and horrified Roger washed her thorn-lacerated legs, forced brandy between her blue lips, and for the first time in their married life laid down the law.

"This damned monkey business has got to stop, Helma. I thought that now, with the baby coming, you'd show some sense. Now, listen. You're going to a doctor, today, if you have to be carried. You're going to stay in the house, nights, if I have to lock you in. I know women act funny when they're pregnant, but you act clean crazy, and it's got to stop." For the first time her tears and pleas had no effect on him; he spooned hot milk between her chattering teeth, and continued, thin-lipped, "One more trick like this—just one, Helma—and we move back to Albany, at least till after the baby comes. Helma, if I have to have you examined by a psychiatrist, maybe—" he could not, although he wanted to, form the threat he had intended. Helma suffered enough in a house. Her acute claustrophobia would certainly kill her in a hospital.

But the threats he had already made had been effective enough to terrify Helma into submission. She saw the doctor, as he stipulated, and reacted quite normally when he assured her that he believed she would have twins. As the winter settled in earnest, the house took on the air of tranquil peace which only the happily pregnant woman knows how to create around the home she has made. As in everything else, Helma was almost animal in this; Roger had never known a woman to seem so healthy, so casual. The wives of his friends fretted and were ungainly and unlovely and given to whims and complaints, and for the first time Roger could favorably compare his wife's docility with theirs. The winter sneaked by on quiet-running feet. Snow came heavy that year, but the roads were kept plowed, and Roger managed to get back and forth every day. If Helma sometimes walked in the woods during the daytime, Roger did not know it, and she never left the house by night. The season was cruelly cold; now and then they could stand at the window and see a deer, made bold by the severity of the season, step out of the forest to the garden gate; and at night wolves howled in the darkness and now and then they heard the fierce snarl of a lynx, far away across the branch. Roger frowned and talked of getting a rifle, but Helma protested, "Wolves are cowards. They never attack anything bigger than a rabbit. And a lynx never bothered anybody who wasn't pokin' around him."

In February Bob Connor shot a lynx, less than a mile from the Lassiter house, and brought it over his shoulder to the door, thumping gaily till they came to look.

"I shot this big fellow down by the rocks on your creek, Roger. Listen, I've been making my kids stay right in the back yard, and if I were you, I wouldn't go in the woods at night, or let your wife. There are a lot of these cats around," he continued, dumping the stiff corpse on the step to ease his shoulder, "And they can be nasty customers—God, Helma, what's the matter! Roger, lookout, " he warned, just in time for Roger to catch Helma as she slumped in a dead faint.

When she had been carried into the bedroom and revived, and had apologized shakily for being such a fool, Bob, out of earshot, had blamed himself severely.

"I'm sorry, Roger. I guess maybe the blood made her fainty-like. Nell hates seeing dead things. I knowed she was in the family way, too, and I ought to had more sense than barge in like that with an old dead wildcat!"

"I don't think that was it," Roger said, baffled, "Helma's never been squeamish about blood."

"She's a bit odd about wild things, though, ain't she?" Bob asked in a tone discreetly lowered, and Roger, distracted, confessed that she was. He watched

Bob go down the road, feeling something like despair, realizing that Bob Connor would certainly add his bit to the stories—already far too prevalent—of Helma Lassiter's "Queerness." But he had not the heart to reprimand or question Helma, nor to repeat Bob Connor's final words, said in that tactfully-dropped voice, "I wouldn't let her run off into the woods thataway, Roger. I go out a lot, shooting these cats, and wolves—bounty on wolves, you know. I try to be careful, and God! I'd hate to shoot somebody!"

After that day Helma grew even quieter, more subdued, losing even the spasmodic impulse to wander in the woods even in broad daylight. Somewhat alarmed, Roger found himself circuitously urging Helma into the garden, at least out of doors, out of the house which she now haunted, sleeping a great deal by day, but rising at night to prowl sleeplessly with her soft pacing movements through all the rooms. When Roger anxiously questioned her, she answered evasively: she was too tired to go far from the house, and the baby's movements in her body were most troublesome at night, and made her restless. She was heavy now, and her face was fuller, giving the wide-set cheekbones under her thick, tawny level brows a curiously unfathomable, animal, enigmatic look. She spoke little, but she seemed happy and tranquil, apart from her restlessness. Roger believed that Helma was trying consciously to wean herself from her wild ways and that she was silently suffering the torture of claustrophobia, for there seemed a curious disturbed look behind the green eyes, when she thought no one was watching her. Roger knew his young wife to be a strong-willed girl, and believed that she could discipline herself unsparingly.

In March came raging winds and a blizzard that swept down from the Adirondacks in a sort of apocalyptic violence, locking both Lassiters in the house for days. Then, overnight, the snow began to melt; the back of the winter was broken, the creeks overflowed with cool melting rains, and a strange moist green appeared through the soaked dead brownness of the grass. Crows and bluejays racketed in new-plowed fields, and a sweet chirping came from the trees at the edge of the woods. Sometimes now on the damp evenings, when light lingered at sundown, Helma would drag her distorted body to the forest gate and lean there, her face poignant with such longing that Roger, watching, felt a hurting pain and pity seeing his wild thing straining so hard at the leash of love he had finally girded about her heart. The gate was never locked, but Helma never touched her fingers to the light latch. Roger was just as well pleased, for now in the warm nights they often heard the snarl and spit of the big wildcats, and in these spring days he knew, the females would be defending their young. Nor did Roger fail to wonder if Helma would likewise be violent hi defence of her child.

He had assumed that when the time came for her confinement he would drive her to the hospital in Albany. She did not say that she approved this arrangement, but on the other hand, she made no protest, and Roger took it for granted.

One evening in late March, while they sat at supper, Helma said quietly "You better drive to Albany and get some coffee, Roger. I used the last for breakfast this morning, and there's none for tomorrow's breakfast."

Like many pliant and easygoing men, Roger was crotchety in small and unimportant trifles, and he scolded Helma with as much severity as he ever used to her; why hadn't she told him at breakfast? She just looked back at him with her closed and heavy face.

"You better go now, or the stores are all going to be closed before you get there."

She was walking around the room restlessly, now and again stopping to pick up some small object and examine it meticulously, handle it with a curious, fidgety stroking movement of her small, rather stubby fingers, then put it impatiently down and resume her feline prowling, "But do you mind if I don't ride along? I'll stay here and go-go to bed. I'm awful tired."

Roger protested. "I don't like to leave you alone, specially at night. Suppose the baby started to come?"

"Well, you'll be back in an hour," Helma said reasonably.

"For heaven's sake, sit down, you'll drive me crazy, pacing like that—" Roger snapped at her, "Are you going to start your fool tricks again?"

"Oh, Roger, please," she started to sob, "I don't think I could stand being bounced around, until I have to!"

The man felt like a brute. Why, he wondered, should he get in a dither, because a girl in the last month of pregnancy didn't want to take a twenty-mile ride in an old car, over the worst roads in New York State? He shrugged and went to the closet for his coat.

"AH right, honey," he said tenderly. "Would you like me to get Mrs. Connor to come and sit with you while I'm gone?"

Helma said in a tone of intense disgust, "Look. I'm twenty-seven years old."

Roger hugged her. "Oh, all right, all right. I'll be back in an hour." He went to the garage to back out the car, but on another thought, ran back up the steps.

"Helma?"

"Yes? I thought you'd gone!"

"You sure you don't want to ride along, or come and stay to Nell Connor's place while I'm gone? I can pick you up on the way back."

Hernia's clear laugh raised staccato echoes in the unlighted porch. "Who's pregnant, you or me? Go along with you, or you'll have to drive all over town to find a store open!"

The muddy roads were now nearly clean of snow, and Roger made good time on the way to Albany. On the edge of town he found a small all-night grocery and decided to go in there, and turn back at once, instead of driving to the uptown chain-store where they usually traded. He bought the coffee and hurried out to the car again, forgetting his change, and only realizing when half-way home again that it had been a five-dollar bill.

It was already dark. Roger, his headlights sweeping a beam across the dark edges of the woods, pictured Helma, curled up kitten-fashion under quilts, but somehow the mental picture held no conviction nor comfort, and he pressed down the accelerator to the floorboard. If a state trooper caught up with him, he'd tell the truth. His wife was pregnant and he didn't like to leave her alone after dark. If it came to that, he'd rather pay a fine than leave her alone any longer.

The house was dark. Only the reflection of his headlights made ghosts on the unlighted window, and then Roger Lassiter saw that the garden gate swung open on its hinges, and that Helma's brown oxfords and crumpled duty socks lay in the mud beside the open gate. At that sight Roger Lassiter's terror jumped up from behind the wall of consciousness, and caught him by the throat. One last wild hope still beat with the thudding of his pulse; Helma might have felt her labor imminent and run to Connor's—the path through the woods was shorter than the road. Like a crazy man he jumped into the auto and sent it careening wildly down the mud road. Before it had fully come to a stop before the Connor farmhouse, he flung the door open and pelted toward the kitchen door entrance. Through the lighted window a Connor child saw him coming, and flung the door open.

"Mommy, here's Mister Lassiter!"

Nell Connor's horsy kind face peered over her child's head. "Roger, come in! What's wrong?"

The man stood blinking numbly in the light. "Is Helma here?"

"Helma? Why, no, Roger! I saw you drive by, earlier, and thought perhaps her time had come and you was takin' her to the hospital!"

"She's gone," Roger said numbly, "She's gone. I drove to Albany to get a pound of coffee, and she said she was too tired to come along. And when I come back she's just gone!

Where's Bob?"

"He went out to hunt lynxes, he said it was full moon and the big cats would prowl all night—oh, my God, Roger!" Nell Connor's pleasant florid face was drained of color, "S'pose Helma's in the woods!" She lowered her voice, glancing at the children, "Bob told me last year that she run off in the woods sometimes, and he said he was scared to hunt. But this winter he's figured that with the baby coming, she'd stay right close to the house."

She was reaching for a man's mackinaw that hung behind the stove, as she spoke.

"Molly," she said to the oldest girl, "You put Kenneth and Edna to bed, now. Miz. Lassiter's lost in the woods, and I'm going to help Mister Lassiter look for her. Donny, you get a lantern and come along. An' Molly, after you get the kids to bed, you make up tots of hot coffee, mind, and you put a couple of hot-water bottles in my bed and put on both teakettles to boil." She explained in an undertone, "If the baby started to come, Helma's kind of nervous, she might get scared to death and just run off and get lost trying to come down here, poor thing. If she did, and the baby started to come, we'll bring her back here. I've had five, I reckon I could kind of look after her."

"You're so good—" Roger faltered.

"Oh, shucks, what's neighbors for? I s'pect Helma'd worry 'bout me, if I got lost." She beckoned to her oldest boy, and took the lantern from his hand.

"We'll go down the path, Donnie. You take the flashlight, and go down the back pasture, 'hind the barn. Keep yelling for your Dad, now. And if you find Miz. Lassiter, you yell like crazy and keep on hollering till we hear you, and then come back and tell Molly to come an' help you get her in the house. Hurry up, now."

Never afterward in his life could Roger remember anything of the next few hours except plodding through moonlit darkness, with the lantern bobbing dully in his hand and Nell Connor's staunch and confident voice growing gradually tired and afraid. They shouted "Hel-ma! Hel-ma! Hel-ma!" until their lips were cracked with cold and their throats hoarse, stopping to listen for answering shouts, and Mrs. Connor faltered, "I dunno how Helma could come so far, being big like she was!" They trembled when they heard an animal snarl in the woods; and once Nell Connor—steady, nerveless Nell, a farm woman all her life, fifty years old—screamed aloud as she saw green eyes and ears laid flat, peering down from a low branch. But worse than this were the times when they heard the distant crack! of a rifle and knew that Bob Connor had shot. Behind Roger's burning eyes was the picture of Helma lying still and stiff beside the path somewhere, shot by accident, or, overcome by travail, lying somewhere in agony, unable to come to them, too far away to hear their shouts and calls, or—worse—hearing, and too weak to answer.

Roger wandered into a dark nightmare, which suddenly dissolved around him as a shout sounded in his ears; his heart stopped and began painfully to beat again, for it seemed that he had heard Helma cry out—Helma, screaming, not far away—He caught at Nell's arm.

"Did you hear that?"

"I heard a catbird or something—" she said doubtfully. "It's Helma! Oh, come on!"

"Roger!" She gripped and held him fast, "I didn't hear anything. Go easy, now. Hark, I heard something—steps—I think it's Bob." She raised her voice, shouting "Bob! Helma! Helma—!"

Out of the night came the harsh snapping CRACK! of rifle fire, close at hand; two shots in rapid succession, then a crashing in the thickets, and Bob Connor lumbered out of the brushwood.

"Nell! Roger! For God's sake, what's the matter! You look like—has something happened to Helma?"

"She's gone—"

"Christ!" said Bob Connor simply. "How long you been hunting her?"

"All night. Bob, I just heard her scream! She's back in there—" Roger gabbled like a madman, "I heard her, and something else—like a baby crying—"

"Easy, easy, Roger!" Bob Connor, his big face compassionate, caught his arm, "I shot a 'cat. A big female, just had cubs. I couldn't leave the little things to die without their mom, so I shot 'em, too."

"It's Helma! Helma's back in there, dying! Let me go, damn it, let me go—" He twisted away from Bob's restraining hands and ran toward the thicket. The Connors followed, breaking into a run after him, catching up as he stopped over the body of the dead lynx.

It was a large female, not yet stiff, tawny gold in color, with strange eyes, and the limp newborn cubs were still wet with slime, unlicked. Roger stood a moment, numbly, over the big graceful still body; then slumped. Bob Connor stepped to put an arm about his shoulders and held him up.

"Come on, Roger. Come on, come on back to the house, you're worn out. Come on. Don't worry. We'll find Hernia. When we get back to the house, you have some coffee, and you look like you could use a shot of whisky. Come on. You're beat right out, man." While he talked, he was urging Roger's limp steps toward the path, "The minute we get to the house," he said soothingly, "I'll get right in the car and go get the state troopers. They'll look all over. Maybe she wandered across to one of the other farms. They'll find her, Roger. Come on."

Roger jerked up his head and looked into Bob Connor's eyes with the blank stare of a man who has been hit and does not know it yet.

"It's no use, Bob. Helma's dead. I know she's dead."

He dropped his head then and began to cry harshly. Over his head, Bob and Nell Connor exchanged grave, sympathetic glances. "He's worn right out.

Come on, Roger, Lean on me. Come on, now, fellow.
. . ."

And where I grew up, they end the story there, because Helma Lassiter never came back. All the farm folks wonder, sometimes, whatever happened to the poor crazy girl.

I used to ride my bike past the Lassiter house that summer and see Mister Lassiter just sitting on his back porch, day after day, just looking off into the woods. The lawn went to rack and ruin, and the rabbits used to hop right up into the garden where he was sitting. And my Daddy never would let me go into the woods looking for nuts again, unless he could go with me with a gun.